Kestrels 4

2̶3

Pony Club Rider

Other Patricia Leitch stories you will enjoy

The Kestrels series

The Jinny series

Kestrels 4

Pony Club Rider

Patricia Leitch

Illustrated by Elsie Lennox

Lions

An Imprint of HarperCollinsPublishers

First published in Great Britain in Lions in 1993

3 5 7 9 10 8 6 4 2

Lions is an imprint of HarperCollins Children's Books,
a division of HarperCollins Publishers Ltd,
77–85 Fulham Palace Road,
Hammersmith, London W6 8JB

Text copyright © Patricia Leitch 1993
Illustrations copyright © Elsie Lennox 1993

The author asserts the moral right to
be identified as the author of this work

ISBN 0 00 694372-1

The author asserts the moral right to
be identified as the author of this work

Printed and bound in Great Britain by
HarperCollins Manufacturing, Glasgow

Chapter One

Sally Lorimer and Thalia ("rhymes-with-
dahlia-which-is-a-flower-like-a-chrysanthe-
mum") Nisbet sat in the back of Mr
Lorimer's car as he drove them through
the grey light of an early autumn evening.
Meg, the Lorimers' elderly bearded collie,
sat in the front bracing her feet against
the car seat as Mr Lorimer swung the car
round the swerves and bends of the country
road.

They were going to Ashdale where Mrs
Blair lived. She was the District Commis-
sioner of the Tarentshire branch of the
Pony Club. Tonight she was holding a
branch meeting to decide who would be

in the Tarent Pony Club team for the Pony Club Junior One-Day-Event in October.

Sally and Thalia were too tense with excitement and nerves even to speak to each other. In two hours' time they would know. The team would have been chosen.

I haven't a chance, Sally told herself. Mrs Blair would never choose me. She groaned aloud in suspense.

Both Sally and Thhhalia were nine years old. Sally was of middling size with thick brown hair that grew straight to her shoulders and was cut in a fringe. Her blue eyes were wide-set and her mouth twisted up at the corners as if she was just about to burst out laughing.

Thalia was tall and lean with fizzing, corn-coloured hair. She lived with her narg, which is gran spelt backwards, in a cottage close to the shore. When her parents had divorced they had given Thalia a roan pony called Tarquin. He was almost thoroughbred and could gallop faster than gale-blown cloud shadows across the sea. The faster Tarquin galloped the better Thalia liked it. She rode him effortlessly, sitting tight and neat as

Tarquin flew over cross-country obstacles or bright show jumps. Both Mrs Blair and Martine Dawes, the head instructress at Mr Frazer's posh riding school, disapproved of Thalia's wild galloping.

Bet you, Thalia told herself, they won't pick me because I'm too fast. But you need a fast pony for cross-country. You need a pony like Tarquin who isn't afraid of jumping strange obstacles.

The Lorimer family had come to live at Kestrels six months ago. Kestrels was a huge stone house. It was built on its own peninsula of land jutting out into the sea, only joined to the mainland by a long, broad avenue lined with copper beech trees.

Mr Lorimer was a librarian. Mrs Lorimer did her best to be a busy housewife but she much preferred wandering about looking at things and painting in watercolours and inks. Ben Lorimer was sixteen. He was tall for his age with a shock of black hair like his father's. He spent most of his time reading. Emma Lorimer was twelve. She had long fair hair and could sing and dance as easily as she could breathe. Jamie was the youngest

Lorimer. He was four and liked mice. They had two dogs. Meg was a twelve-year-old black and white bearded collie and Misty, a grey and white beardie, was eight.

They had all fallen in love with Kestrels when they had first discovered it, empty, neglected and drowning in an overgrown garden.

Although they had all ached to live in it they knew they could never afford to buy it. Then Mr Lorimer's Great-Uncle Nathan died in Australia. Mr Lorimer had hardly known him but since Great-Uncle Nathan had no family of his own he left Mr Lorimer a considerable amount of money and their dream came true. They all came to live at Kestrels.

Before she came to Kestrels Sally had only ridden at Miss Meek's riding school. Up and down, up and down Miss Meek's lane on aged ponies who tripped over their hooves and ignored their riders, while they dreamt of meadows beside slow-flowing rivers where they could roll and graze in freedom.

Sally had met Thalia when her family came to see round Kestrels before they bought it. Sally's first ride on Tarquin had been a disaster. Tarquin, knowing that Sally was not in control, had galloped madly across the sands leaping the breakwater, then swung round to race back to Thalia with Sally clinging on to his mane – a helpless passenger.

But that had been before she rescued Willow from a meat man. Willow was a dapple-grey mare with a dished Araby face and huge, dark, Arab eyes. Her silver mane lay over her arched neck and her tail fell over strong-boned hocks. She was completely reliable and gradually Sally had learnt to trust her; to gallop and jump, until at last weekend's Tarent Show she and Willow had been first with Thalia and Tarquin in the cross-country pairs class. Mrs Blair had been at the show and after seeing them jump had asked them both to join the Pony Club and be considered for the Junior One-Day-Event team.

But she won't pick me. I know she won't. She'll only want to borrow Willow for someone else to ride. She'll remember how nervous I was. She'll never pick me, Sally told herself as Mr Lorimer stopped the car in front of Ashdale. Immediately the front door opened and Mr Blair was welcoming them in.

"Come along in. Come along. You are the last. Mr Lorimer? So good of you to bring them. Where would the Pony Club be without its parents? That's what I say. Now, coffee is laid on for parents. Of course bring in the old dog too. We'll find a rug for her. Girls, down that way to the study. They're waiting for you."

Before she knocked on the solid oak door Thalia swallowed hard. "They must pick us. They must," she swore through clenched teeth.

Sally shuddered, suddenly seeing impossible cross-country obstacles looming in front of her and hearing show jumps crashing down behind Willow because Sally had ridden her wrongly at the jump. But that was in the past.

"We must be in the team," she vowed and for that second she didn't think about letting the team down or falling off, but only of the magical, glorious moment when the

Tarentshire branch with Thalia and herself in the team were presented with the cup.

"In you come," called Mrs Blair. Thalia opened the door to a comfortably furnished room lit by table lamps and the flames from a log fire. The grey evening was shut out by heavy velvet curtains and the walls garlanded with streamers of rosettes. Mrs Blair was short and thick-set and Martine Dawes was young, dark and dashing. They sat together on a settee with a coffee table covered with Pony Club folders and papers in front of them.

"Now, find yourselves a place and I'll let you all know what we have decided," Mrs Blair told them.

There were seven other children in the study sitting in the huge armchairs or on cushions on the floor. Sally and Thalia only recognised three of the girls and one boy by sight, but they knew Simon Knowles. Simon was a brilliant rider, but after a fall on a cross-country course when he had broken both his legs and his pony Merlin, who also broke a leg, had to be shot, he had refused to jump again. It was not until Tarent Show when Sally had persuaded Simon's father to buy Clover, one of Miss Meek's riding school ponies, that Simon had begun to regain his confidence.

Verity Blair, one of Mrs Blair's daughters, was sitting astride the arm of a settee. She rode Buster, a solid bay pony that had been passed down through the family.

Charlotte Main was there. She was one of Thalia's and Sally's most unfavourite persons.

"Bet the spotty Charlotte will be picked," Thalia whispered to Sally. "Ignore her if she comes near us."

"Right," said Mrs Blair standing up. "Great to see you all here. I should love to tell you that you are all going to be possibles for the team but that cannot be. We have picked six possibles. After the six have been training for a few weeks Martine and I will pick the four who will make up our team. This year the branch event is at Leighton Hall on the third Saturday in October. So we have a lot of hard riding to do before then."

"Oh, Mum!" interrupted Verity. "We are all desperate to know who you've chosen."

"This very second I shall put you all out of your misery." Mrs Blair reached for a typewritten list of names. "Martine and I have given a lot of careful consideration to this list. But, remember, the ones who have not been picked, there is always next year . . .

"Verity is in. Not because she is my daughter but because we need Buster as our anchor. He has been to several events and he knows what it's all about.

"Simon, I hear you have a new pony?"

"Dad bought her yesterday. She's super." But Simon's face didn't show any enthusiasm.

"We were a bit worried about you. Didn't think Clover would have the stamina. But with a new pony you're a possible. You are in."

As she listened Sally felt the warm room change to arctic winter. If Simon had a new pony what would happen to Clover? Would his father sell her? Might she end up back at Miss Meek's riding school?

"Third rider," continued Mrs Blair, "is Charlotte Main. We have chosen you after a lot of thought. If you are repeatedly late for practices you will not be in the team, no matter how well Pie is jumping. Understood?"

Charlotte scowled but nodded. "I'm the best rider here," she began, but Mrs Blair ignored her.

"Brian Green," she said to the boy Sally and Thalia didn't know. "How is Punch?"

"Fine," said Brian, pushing his curly brown hair out of his eyes and looking away from Mrs Blair.

"Then brush him down, wake him up and bring him along to Saturday's practice."

"Oh, thanks. Thank you," said Brian in an amazed voice.

Only Sally, Thalia and the three girls they didn't know were left.

"Thalia, you are in. We hope you will see sense and steady Tarquin. We don't want a broken neck, neither yours nor the pony's. So slow down."

"I will. I promise I will," beamed Thalia, but in her mind's eye she was already galloping Tarquin over drops and ditches at flat-out speed.

Sally dug her nails into the palms of her hands. The three girls she didn't know all looked far more competent than herself. They all looked as if they had been riding for years.

"Last team member... Sally, we've chosen you. Martine thinks you have improved tremendously since you've been riding Willow. This is your chance. Keep on improving and you are in the team."

Sally and Thalia beamed at each other. They were both in.

"But of course," said Charlotte to no one in particular, "the trouble will start if she comes off Willow and won't get on again."

Mrs Blair ignored her but Sally blushed scarlet. Before she had Willow she had fallen off one of Mr Frazer's ponies and refused to get on again. Charlotte had been there. But it had all been months ago. Sally had almost forgotten about it. Only someone as beastly as Charlotte would have mentioned it.

Mrs Blair spoke briefly about the one-day-event, explaining that it was a small branch event, with five teams competing. There would be a simple dressage test, a cross-country course and then showjumping.

They would all have a lot to do before October. The first team practice was at Ashdale next Saturday, one o'clock prompt. Martine would instruct. She looked forward to seeing them all.

"See you tomorrow," Thalia shouted, waving goodbye when Mr Lorimer had dropped her off at her narg's cottage. "Got to start getting them fit."

"Sounds like hard labour," said Sally's father as he drove off.

"It will be," replied Sally nodding contentedly. It was beyond all her dreams to have been picked for a Pony Club team and she didn't care how hard she had to work.

Suddenly Sally glimpsed a silver-white shape standing close to the hedge. It was a white greyhound. Caught in the glare of the headlights it seemed a magical glimmering being. It had long, delicate legs, a tight-muscled body, arched neck and a fine-boned head. Any other dog's eyes would have shone red or green in the headlights, but the white hound's eyes gleamed like luminous, rose-coloured crystal.

Sally caught her breath at this sudden glimpse of beauty; at this gift from the dark.

"Stop!" she shouted. "Look! In the hedge. There's a dog ..." But her father had no intention of stopping.

Telling her family that she had been chosen as a possible for the team filled up the rest of Sally's evening and it wasn't until she was sitting on the window seat in her bedroom looking out over the sea that Sally remembered the strange white hound.

Before they bought Kestrels the Lorimers had been for a picnic in Fintry Bay close to Kestrels. They were packing up to go home to Matwood when Sally had wandered down to the sea's edge by herself. She had seen something glinting in the water and had crouched down to find out what it was. As she reached her hand out into the sea the waves had swept a tiny crystal unicorn into her open palm.

It was just after this that they had heard about Mr Lorimer's inheritance. Then they had come to live at Kestrels, Sally had made friends with Thalia and she had found

Willow. Sally was sure that it was a magic unicorn. She always kept it in her pocket or standing on the windowsill in her bedroom where the sea light danced rainbows around it.

"We're both in the team, least in as possibles," Sally whispered holding the unicorn in the palm of her hand. Suddenly she remembered the silver-white hound that had stood so still as they drove past. There had been a magic about it too – a calm stillness that echoed in Sally's mind; a silver-rose hound touched with unicorn magic.

Chapter Two

Simon's new pony burst out of the Knowles' trailer into the stable yard at Ashdale like an exploding space rocket. Simon, clutching at her halter rope, raced beside her.

"There's a pony for you!" roared Mr Knowles. "That's a pony worth riding. Cost me the best part of two thousand pounds but worth every penny of it. She'll take Simon back to the top where he belongs."

Sally and Thalia were already mounted. Martine had brought them to Ashdale in Mr Frazer's horsebox for the first team practice.

"Whee!" exclaimed Thalia in total admiration, hardly noticing Tarquin's rearing fright.

"What a sheer brill pony! Not as good as Tarquin, of course," she added just in case anyone should have heard her.

Willow pricked neat, surprised ears and watched the display through mild eyes.

Remembering Simon's terrible fall Sally wondered how he would cope with such a lightning pony. It was only a few days since Simon had been unwilling to ride Clover at the Tarent Show and now his father had bought him a mad runaway pony to ride.

Sally had phoned Simon to make sure that they would not sell Clover. Simon had assured her that they would never, ever dream of selling Clover for it was Clover that had given him back his confidence and she would have a home with them for always. But Sally couldn't be sure.

A stupid pony to buy for Simon, she decided. His father must be a bit mad.

Simon, with no sign of nerves, had jumped into the saddle and was walking the black pony around on a loose rein; speaking quietly to her; giving her time to settle.

"I do not believe it," groaned Martine to Mrs Blair. "Just when Simon has started riding again that idiot of a father had to buy him a pony like that!"

Mrs Blair nodded her head in agreement.

"Everyone," called Martine, clapping her hands to gain attention. "Down to the paddock."

Simon and Thalia led the way on high-trotting ponies. Next, Verity sitting securely on Buster with Sally riding beside her and trying not to look at the cross-country obstacles which seemed to grow bigger the more she looked at them. Brian Green on a shaggy, ungroomed, native pony rode behind them while a handful of parents brought up the rear.

They had been schooling for nearly half an hour when Charlotte, riding her piebald, came trotting full out down to the paddock.

"It was all Mum's fault," she shouted. "I kept telling her to get a move on and then the flippin' phone rang and she gossiped for hours."

Martine ignored her and Mrs Blair looked pointedly at her watch but said nothing.

They schooled for another ten minutes and then left their ponies with the parents while they walked round eight squashed-down cross-country obstacles with Martine showing them the correct way to take each obstacle.

"I think," said Thalia to Sally, "that if your pony is going fast enough you can clear anything."

"Well, you would, wouldn't you!" snapped Martine, overhearing Thalia. "But you are WRONG. I am here to tell you the correct way to ride a cross-country course. Please have the manners to listen."

Thalia did not apologise. When it was her turn to ride she went round the jumps at a blazing gallop, soaring high and clear over all the jumps.

Willow took Sally round at a careful canter.

"A little more speed?" suggested Mrs Blair. "Perhaps if you stood next to Thalia you might blend together and you could both jump at a medium pace."

Simon struggled to control Zodiac, but her head was up and she charged the jumps, throwing herself over them in a furious fandango of mane, tail and flying hooves.

"She needs a martingale and no more cross-country," warned Martine. "Cavaletti and trotting in circles until you've balanced her up."

Buster, who knew the course well, popped round with a flick of his tail. Mrs Blair told her daughter off for not kicking him on.

Punch, Brian Green's pony, trotted up to the first three obstacles and ducked round them. At the fourth jump – a brush fence – he swung round and belted back to the other ponies.

Charlotte rode over the course smoothly and efficiently, her piebald accurately timing his take-offs and landings. Going at a steady gallop she made nothing of the small jumps and rode back to the others with a superior expression on her face.

"Well done," said Martine. Turning to Thalia she added, "That's how Tarquin would jump if you would only let him settle."

"I wouldn't want Tarquin to jump like that. Tarquin cleared them all and he was ten billion times faster than Pie," said Thalia answering back.

Martine's reply was drowned by Mrs Blair as she instructed everyone to go over to the showjumping paddock.

"Let's make it a race," Charlotte challenged as they rode down to the show jumps. "Whoever is fastest is the winner."

"Don't be daft," said Sally. "We're here to practise for the team. The one-day-event isn't a speed competition." But she saw Simon grinning and passing on the dare to Thalia.

Simon jumped first. He winked at Charlotte as he rode into the field with its precise arrangement of show jumps. They were to ride over four jumps round the outside of the paddock and then down the centre over parallel poles.

Thalia stood up in her stirrups, bright with excitement as she watched Simon and Zodiac race round the outside jumps. Zodiac increased her speed at every jump. By the time she came charging down the centre of the paddock Simon, his face set, was pulling helplessly at his reins. Zodiac slipped as she took off, almost skidded into the poles, then leapt hopelessly high and landed on the middle of the jump. There was a crash of breaking poles and Simon was thrown to the ground as Zodiac, high-stepping as a spider in water, fought to free herself from the wreckage.

For a second everyone seemed to hold their breath. Then Mrs Blair was running to Simon shouting to him not to get up and Martine rushed to catch Zodiac.

"Nothing to make a fuss about," shouted Simon's father. "Boy's used to taking a toss." But for once his usual bossy expression had changed to one of concern.

Sally sat on Willow watching helplessly. There was nothing she could do. She could only watch and wait. Wait to see if Simon would remount and jump again.

Martine checked Zodiac and found nothing wrong with her. Simon scrambled to his feet.

"Nothing broken?" asked Mrs Blair, making Simon move his arms and legs and wriggle his fingers and toes.

"I'm fine," said Simon but Sally, watching intently, saw the fear in his eyes, his tucked-in lips. Then he straightened his shoulders and drew in his breath, forcing himself to ride again.

He took Zodiac from Martine, mounted and cantered her in a circle and before his father had time to shout at him he had turned Zodiac and ridden over the four jumps around the paddock. In spite of her crash Zodiac cleared them easily and this time Simon managed to control her speed.

"Good boy," praised Mrs Blair. "Well done. Now, no more jumping until we steady her up. Sitting trot and patience."

"OK," said Simon, a sudden smile of relief lighting his tense face.

"She's got a good jump in her," said Martine. "I'll come over and help you. We'll soon get her sorted out."

Thalia was next.

"You've seen for yourself what happens when you let a pony tear round out of control," Mrs Blair told her, and for once Thalia had nothing to say.

She nodded, not looking at Mrs Blair, but still sent Tarquin sailing on over the jumps.

Charlotte had two refusals. She rode back scowling, making Sally think that if Mrs Blair hadn't been there she would have been using her riding whip in temper.

Buster popped round obligingly and Brian on Punch had eight refusals.

Sally was still so shaken by Simon's fall that she forgot that this was jumping and she should be feeling nervous. Without thinking about it she sat easily over the jumps, going with her pony.

"Very nice," said Martine. "You have remembered the things I taught you."

"But I wasn't even thinking about what I should be doing," gasped Sally, suddenly feeling guilty.

"That's even better," laughed Martine. "You were doing what came naturally."

It was late afternoon before Sally and Thalia were sitting next to Martine in the horsebox driving home to Kestrels, Tarquin and Willow safely tied in the box behind them.

Mrs Blair had handed out typed sheets giving each of them details of feeding, exercise and the dates of future team practices, and told them that they all had a long way to go before they could even begin to think of themselves as a team.

Martine drove quickly through the gathering grey dusk, chatting about past events and the horses she had ridden. They had almost reached the turn-off for Kestrels when Martine jammed her foot on the brake, bringing the horsebox to a violent halt.

"Glory be!" she shouted as she threw herself out of the cabin. "Never saw it. Another second and I'd have been over it!"

Sally and Thalia scrambled out with her.

"What?" demanded Thalia. "What was it?"

"Dog," said Martine. "Big white dog. Don't know how I missed it. It ran straight in front of me."

"There it is!" cried Sally, and she pointed to where the white hound was standing on the other side of the road. It was the hound she had glimpsed from her father's car.

The hound stood perfectly still. Her delicate bones, long, fragile-seeming legs, sickle tail, sweet reach of neck and delicate head gave her a strange beauty. She watched them through her pale eyes as they crossed the road towards her.

"Lord, that was a near thing! She's invisible in this light," said Martine.

Sally reached out her hand to stroke the hound but hesitated. Somehow it seemed wrong to touch her. She wasn't that kind of dog. Unlike the beardies who leapt and bounced over everyone they met, the white hound had a cool distance about her, a centre of silence that made Sally draw back.

Two men burst through the hedge behind the horsebox. They were both roughly dressed in muddied boots and worn jackets.

"Here, you!" one of them shouted. "Leave the bloomin' dog alone. Don't you go petting a dog like that one. Wait till I get her."

He knotted the dirty rope he was carrying round the hound's neck.

"You keep your hands off of it," he said.

"You should have had her on a lead," Martine told them sharply. "Think yourselves lucky I didn't run her over. No dog should be running loose like that."

The man grunted, yanked at the rope and, dragging the white hound behind him, he and his companion walked off, away from Kestrels. The white hound's movements were filled with grace as she trotted beside the shambling humans.

"She can't belong to them," cried Sally, watching them go.

"But she does," stated Thalia. "They're staying in the cottage at Mr Palmer's farm, working for him. She's their dog."

"They don't deserve to have a dog like that," said Sally bitterly. "They must have stolen her from somewhere."

Mrs Lorimer and Emma had put down beds for the ponies, who were in at night now, then filled hay nets and water buckets. When the ponies were settled and eating their feeds Martine came back to Kestrels for a coffee.

"Narg's here," Mrs Lorimer told Thalia, who followed them across the grass to the house.

Sally waited for a moment to watch Willow eating her feed. She loved to see her secure and settled against the night.

"You were the best pony," Sally told her before she swung away to race after the others.

She had almost caught up with them when she saw that Misty was leaping round Martine, but there was no sign of Meg. Sally looked back and saw Meg making her way slowly towards her.

"Come on then," Sally cried. "Did we leave you behind?"

Meg trotted a few stiff steps then fell back into a walk.

"It's all right. I'm waiting for you," Sally told her.

As she stood silently in the gathering dark she put her hand into her jacket pocket, cradling the crystal unicorn, and with her dreaming eye she saw the unicorn stepping between the dark gold and pearl of silver birch trees, the white hound by its side.

Chapter Three

September settled into solid rain. Fields were flooded and the gateway to the ponies' field was churned into a swamp of mud.

Martine came out to Kestrels and trace-clipped Willow and Tarquin.

"I haven't taken too much off," she said when she had finished clipping. "Just under their tums and chest."

"Please, please, couldn't you clip all of Tarquin? He would look like a race-pony, a thoroughbred. I've always longed to see him clipped out and poshed. Please?"

"You'll have enough to do coping with New Zealand rugs – filthy, muddy, soaking wet New Zealand rugs – but they do mean that your ponies can go out during the day. You don't have to exercise them if the weather is too appalling."

"Oh, but we will exercise them," said Sally. "Mrs Blair's instructions say that we have to exercise every day, road work at a walk and sitting trot."

"Good on you," said Martine. "Wish I had your energy."

In the mornings and after school Sally and Thalia rode through the rain.

"We need goggles with windscreen wipers," Sally said as she kicked Willow on into the deluge.

" 'Wind and water women'," quoted Thalia, sitting tightly on Tarquin as he reared trying to escape from the driving rain and gallop back to Kestrels.

Mr Lorimer had persuaded Thalia's narg to let him pay for Tarquin's feeding and anything else that Thalia or her pony might need.

"A good job she agreed," said Thalia. "No way could we ever have afforded all this feeding and rugs. Your father is my wizard godfather."

"Perhaps your parents would have paid something?" suggested Sally.

"My dad can hardly afford a flippin' birthday card," said Thalia. "I get all knotted up in case my father appears and wants to take Tarquin away and sell him."

"He couldn't do that!" exclaimed Sally.

"J-O-K-E joke," said Thalia, but Sally thought that it wasn't altogether a joke.

One Saturday was so wet that Mrs Blair phoned them to tell them to leave their ponies at home and only bring themselves to Ashdale. When they were all sitting round the table in Mrs Blair's study she gave out cards for them to keep with a diagram of the dressage arena marked on them and details of the dressage test for the Junior Event. They began by saluting the judge from the middle of the arena and then had to ride different movements stopping and starting at the different letters marked outside the arena.

"It is quite simple," said Mrs Blair. "Remember that."

"When can we practise it?" asked Charlotte, who had arrived late and was making up for it by asking bossy questions.

"Never," said Mrs Blair. "We will ride all the different figures in the test but not in the correct order. You will ride it only once before the event. If you ride the test only a few times your pony begins to know what he has to do next. It's called anticipating and is a real no-no! So walk the test on your feet, walk it with your fingers round a table and ride it in your mind every spare second. You must wear gloves when you are riding the test. When you salute the judge you have your reins in one hand, your other hand is down by your side and you salute by nodding your head."

"The dressage is the worst," said Martine as she drove them home. "I love the cross-country and the showjumping but the dressage – ugh! When I ride into the arena all on my own, my mind just fudges up. I cannot remember a thing. Have no idea where to go."

"Tarquin won't like it," said Thalia. "He hates schooling."

"Or *you* do?" suggested Martine.

Sally was sure Willow would enjoy dressage. Walking, trotting and cantering at the correct letters placed round the arena; being neat and accurate. And, thought Sally, nothing to be afraid of.

But she pushed the thought out of her head for that didn't matter now. She was not afraid now.

That evening Sally and Em went down to say goodnight to the ponies. Misty was in the kitchen helping Mr Lorimer with the washing-up by gulping down the scraps before he washed the plates. But Meg came with them, getting out of her basket in a stiff, bumbling hurry, her face anxious in case she was going to be left behind.

Tarquin was still pulling at strands of hay caught in his haynet while Willow lay like a cuddly toy snug in her bed of deep straw. Even when Sally and Emma looked in over her half-door she didn't get to her feet.

"So lucky," said Sally, her spine shivering with delight as she laid her arms along the box door and rested her chin on her arms. "A pony of my own, Thalia and Tarquin, and living here."

"And being in the Pony Club team," added Em, half teasing, half agreeing.

"Might not be," said Sally. "Mrs Blair still has to pick *the* team. Two of us will be dropped. Only four in the real team. Mrs Blair is telling us next week."

"What will you do if Thalia gets picked and you don't?"

"Die," said Sally, shrugging the possibility away from her. It was an idea so terrible that she didn't dare to think about it.

They went back across the stable yard. Meg had not come with them to the stables but was sitting in the grass panting as she waited for them. As they reached her she got to her feet and followed behind them, her head lifted, following their smell.

"Come on, Meg," Sally shouted, pausing to let Meg catch up with them. "You're a lazy old dog."

Meg broke into a trot, her white, paddy paws flopping up and down.

"That's it," encouraged Sally. But just then Meg stopped suddenly, stood for a moment gasping for breath, then fell over on her side and lay still.

"Meg!" Sally screamed as she dashed to her. "Em, there's something wrong with Meg!"

Meg's eyes were closed, her breathing was harsh and when Sally crouched down beside her, stroking her, she took no notice but lay stretched out in the long grass without moving.

Em ran for their father while Sally waited stroking Meg's dense hair and holding her limp paws.

"She just fell down," Sally told them when Mr Lorimer and Ben came racing towards her. "She's not dead, is she? She's not dead?"

"Of course not," said Mr Lorimer sharply. "Don't know if we should try and move her or not. Ben, phone for the vet."

"Right," said Ben and raced back to the house.

"We'll need to do something," pleaded Sally desperately, tears running down her cheeks. "We can't leave her lying here."

"I don't know. Perhaps . . ." began Mr Lorimer. Even as he spoke Meg gave a sudden shudder and lifted her head.

She looked round with a dazed expression, then stood up, her tail wagging. She took a few steps away from them then looked round, barking to know why they were all standing there instead of getting home to the fire.

"She's better!" exclaimed Em. "Maybe she only wanted a sleep."

"A bit more than that, I'm afraid," said Mr Lorimer. "We'll see what the vet has to say."

Sally reached out for her father's hand and held on to it tightly. Although Meg was walking ahead of them Sally knew there was something wrong. Meg had not just been asleep.

Mr Cheever, the vet, arrived about an hour later. He examined Meg, taking her temperature, looking at her eyes and mouth and listening to her heart.

"She's OK now," he said, giving Meg a last pat before he stood up. "May never happen again. How old is she?"

"Twelve," said Mr Lorimer.

"Fair age," said Mr Cheever.

"It's not!" cried Sally. "It's not very old at all."

Her mother drew Sally to her side, hugging her close while they listened to the vet.

"Maybe you're right," he said to Sally. "She could go on for years. It's her heart. Bit tired. Something wrong for a second when she keeled over. I'll give her an injection, and could someone collect pills for her tomorrow? A good chance you'll never notice anything wrong again. Bring her in to see me in a month."

Sally went slowly up to her room. She did not want Meg to be old. Did not want her to be ill. No matter what the vet said, if it was Meg's heart it must be serious.

Through her window she could see the swell and glint of the sea. The moon threw black shadows and struck a silver radiance from the crystal unicorn standing in its place on the windowsill. Sally stood staring at the unicorn, hardly seeing it, thinking only about Meg. Then a movement outside caught her gaze, and looking through the glass she saw the white hound crossing the lawn.

The hound paused and looked straight at Sally. For a second she stood with her front paw lifted, her sickle tail carving the dark and her strange, pale eyes looking up from her porcelain-fine head. Almost before Sally could be sure she was there she had turned and vanished into the shadows.

Chapter Four

"Of course you didn't see it," stated Thalia as they were setting out next Monday morning to exercise. "It was your imagination. Honestly, the men have been away for ages. The cottage is all locked up."

"Well, the hound is still here. I did see her."

Thalia looked at her watch. "We've just got time before school to ride round by the cottage and then you can see for yourself. OK?"

Before Sally had a chance to disagree Thalia led the way down the track from Kestrels to the shore.

When the ponies felt the sand beneath their hooves they were filled with a longing for speed – Tarquin pranced excitedly by the wave crests and gleaming sands, Willow clinked her bit and gathered herself together – and at exactly the same moment they charged forward.

Sally sat easily as Willow cantered along. Clouds of raucous gulls rose in front of them, wheeling overhead then settling again precisely above their reflections once the ponies had passed.

Too much, thought Sally. Too much happening.

She was sure, absolutely certain, that she had seen the white hound. As certain as she was that Mrs Lee, her teacher, was going to be very annoyed with the messy project that Sally had handed in last week. She had rushed through it so that she would have more time to ride.

Next Saturday was only five days away. Then she would know if she had been picked for the team or not. Too much. Too much.

And then there was Meg. The thought of Meg being ill swept over Sally like a thunder cloud. Nothing must happen to Meg. She must always be there. They wouldn't be a proper family without Meg.

"Buck up," commanded Thalia, "or we're going to be late for school."

Sally eased her reins, letting Willow gallop on, leaving behind her the fear of Meg dying and the dread of Thalia being picked for the team when she had not been chosen.

They rode up past Narg's and along a track to the farmer's cottage.

"See," said Thalia. "Absolutely shut. The men have been away for weeks."

Seeing the padlocked door, the windows shuttered against the winter gales, Sally couldn't argue.

"But who is looking after the hound?" she demanded.

"I expect they took her with them. Must have been another dog you saw," said Thalia, turning Tarquin and trotting him towards the road.

Mrs Lorimer was waiting for them at the stables.

"Where have you been?" she said crossly. "Put your ponies into their boxes and I'll see to them. Your father's waiting for you. For goodness' sake get a move on or he'll have gone without you."

"We had to find out about something. Something really urgent," explained Thalia. "We didn't realise it was so late."

"Thalia, get a move on!" roared Mrs Lorimer, losing her temper. Thalia abandoned Tarquin and raced for Kestrels where she had left her school clothes earlier that morning.

Mrs Lee was not willing to listen to Sally's excuses about her rubbish project on British trees. Mrs Lee thought homework should come before riding and told Sally so, while Sally stood, not hearing a word she said. She was too worried about the white hound. Who would take care of her now that the men had gone?

"I want the whole thing done again and handed in next Monday morning."

By then, Sally thought, we will know who is in the team. It will all be settled. She took her project from Mrs Lee hardly glancing at it.

Next Saturday Sally and Thalia, holding their ponies, stood in the stable yard waiting for Martine to arrive with the horsebox. Although Mrs Blair had told them that she would be picking the team today, that was all she had said. Sally stood leaning against Willow's saddle going over and over the dressage test while Thalia, who hadn't thought too much about the dressage test, was imagining Tarquin soaring over Mrs Blair's show jumps.

"Do you think Mrs Blair will have a competition and the first four will be the team?" Sally asked.

"Nope," said Thalia. "They will have made up their minds by now. They'll not have Punch. Bound to choose Buster and the loathsome, spotty, Charlotte. That leaves Simon, you and me. Two of us in the team. One not."

Thalia's voice went squeaky and she looked away from Sally, staring up the drive, willing the horsebox to appear.

Tarquin must be in the team, she thought. MUST be. And Sally. It wouldn't be any use without Sally.

The horsebox came clattering down the drive. They loaded their ponies and climbed up into the cabin.

"Don't look at me like that," Martine told them. "I don't know who is going to be in the team. It is still in the lap of the gods."

Even when they arrived at Ashdale there was no mention of choosing the team. They schooled and then took it in turns to walk, trot and canter in a circle, change rein and circle again in the opposite direction at the different paces.

Charlotte was so late that she hardly had time to school at all. She came galloping into the paddock, her hard hat stuck on the back of her head, her jacket unbuttoned.

"Hope I haven't missed anything," she yelled. "Not much point in schooling Pie. He knows it all."

If Mrs Blair heard, she said nothing.

When Charlotte had ridden her circles they went for a ride over the hill with Martine riding Mr Blair's grey hunter.

"En-joy, en-joy," Thalia coded to Sally. "We've got all this land to ride in, smashing ponies and you jumped that drop without shifting an inch."

"Enjoy myself!" said Simon overhearing. "Some hope. Zodiac goes bonkers when she gallops and my father will murder me if I'm not in the team. Why hasn't she told us?"

But Sally and Thalia had no time to

answer. Martine was trotting on downhill, checking up on her ride over her shoulder.

Like a pied piper Martine rode ahead of them and they followed where she led – popping over dry stone walls, twisting suddenly to jump a ditch then gallop on over rough moorland. They finished with a long canter, jumping over a pole propped up by a rusty bulk of farm machinery, then slowing to a trot as they swung round the side of the hill.

"That blew the cobwebs away!" said Martine, grinning. She stood up in her stirrups and checked over ponies and riders.

"Oh, again, again," cried Thalia. "That was super!"

They cooled their ponies off by walking them back to Ashdale along the road. When they reached the yard there was no sign of Mrs Blair. It wasn't until they had boxed their ponies that Martine told Brian to put Punch into a loosebox because Mrs Blair wanted to see them, minus muddy boots, for a few minutes in her study.

"This is it," groaned Simon.

"I just hope she doesn't keep us too long," grumbled Charlotte. "I don't see why I should have to wait. Pie is bound to be in the team. I think she should just tell me and let me go."

"Right," said Mrs Blair when they had all found a place to sit. "This is what you have all been waiting for."

Please, thought Sally desperately. Please me.

"You've all done very well, but as you know the team has to consist of four riders, so two of you must go. It wouldn't be fair to you or your ponies to expect you to come to team practices when I know you are not going to be in the team.

"Brian, I'm sorry, but Punch is not fast enough. It would take a stronger rider than you to wake him up, so I'm afraid you are out."

"That's OK, Mrs Blair," said Brian cheerfully. "I'd rather go to the rugby with my dad."

"Verity is in. We need Buster to hold us together.

"Simon, you are in. Let's hope you can

come to terms with Zodiac before the event. At present you both have potential."

"Whee! Thank goodness," said Simon. "My old man would have blown a gasket if you'd dropped us."

"Which leaves us with Charlotte, Thalia and Sally. One of you has got to go."

Mrs Blair paused and the silence in the room was so loud they could all hear it.

"Well, I've decided to keep Thalia in the team."

Thalia gave a gulp of delight and Sally dug her nails even deeper into the palms of her hands.

"But you must steady Tarquin. You are perfectly capable of slowing him down if you want to. Understood?"

Thalia nodded vigorously.

"Now, Charlotte or Sally? Charlotte has been riding a good bit longer than Sally and she has done some competition riding."

Charlotte's face beamed smugly.

"Of course I knew . . ." she began to say to Verity.

"But she has been late for every practice," continued Mrs Blair. "Not the fault of her transport, I've checked with her mother. She has paid next to no attention to Martine's instruction. Has continued to chat when she has been repeatedly told to shut up. In fact she has been an intolerable nuisance for most of the time."

Charlotte's mouth dropped open. She stared furiously at Mrs Blair.

"Sally, on the other hand, has worked and improved both her own riding and her pony. We don't know, perhaps Willow has already been ridden in a one-day-event, but we shall see how she goes in October. I've decided to make Sally the fourth member of the team."

"But that's not fair," stormed Charlotte. "I'm a far better rider than Sally. She's so nervous."

"Quite enough," warned Mrs Blair. "Charlotte and Brian, thank you both for coming. I hope you won't think it has been time wasted. Now I'd like the team to stay on for another minute or two."

Charlotte stamped out. Brian thanked Mrs Blair before he left.

"You are *the* team," Mrs Blair said when they had gone. "For the one-day-event the three top scores will count. That means should anything disastrous happen to one of you the other three MUST complete all three parts of the event or the team is eliminated."

Instantly Sally imagined mucking up the dressage; falling off on the cross-country and knocking everything down in the show-jumping.

"As well as the team cup there is a cup for the best individual. I expect you to win them both!"

"Naturally," said Thalia.

"One last thing before you go. A week next Saturday, that's in a fortnight, we are going to have a mini one-day-event here at Ashdale. I've invited the Haxton Pony Club over for the day. We will ride *the* dressage test, go round some of the cross-country obstacles that your ponies don't know and finish up with showjumping. The real thing. Rosettes for the winners."

"Super!" rejoiced Thalia. "Tarquin will love it."

Simon said nothing. He looked down at his hands spread out on his knees. The

Pony Club Junior One-Day-Event would have been the first cross-country competition he had ridden in since his fall on Merlin when his pony had been killed and he had broken both his legs. A bit of Simon was still terrified. He could still hear the thud as Merlin's hind legs hit the fixed poles, feel Merlin's bulk on top of him and feel the pain in his own legs. He had been counting the days to the Pony Club Event, building up his courage. Now, in just two short weeks, he was to be part of a team again, riding fast over fixed jumps because he couldn't let the team down.

Sally didn't know what to think, whether to be glad to have the chance of riding in a competition before the real thing, or to be shivering at the thought.

"You never told me!" cried Verity. "Oh, Mum, why did you choose the Haxton lot? Why? Why didn't you ask the Penfrew Branch?"

"What are the Haxton Branch like?" Thalia asked Verity.

"Wait and see," said Verity darkly. "You'll know soon enough."

Chapter Five

It was a bright, blue, frosty morning making Sally's toes tingle as she stamped her feet on Ashdale's stable yard and waited for the arrival of the Haxton Pony Club team.

"Wish they'd come," said Verity. "Then we could get mounted. Trust my mother to make us into a welcoming committee."

"Wish I was on Zodiac," Simon agreed. "I feel a right nit standing here like this."

Sally stared about her at all the excitement and bustle. The dressage arena was marked out with white letters.

"Enter at A, trot to X, halt, salute judge, remembering to smile. Walk on to C and turn right . . ." Sally repeated under her breath. She knew the test as well as she knew her two times table.

Parents and friends who were there to help with the organisation walked about with clip boards, stop-watches and biros asking each other if they knew what to do. Narg, Mrs Lorimer, Emma and Jamie were setting up a food centre in the back of an open horsebox.

"Oh, hurry up!" demanded Thalia. "Tarquin will be in a filthy mood being dumped in a loosebox he doesn't know. COME NOW!"

And in answer to Thalia's command a horsebox came roaring up the drive. It was very new. Its chrome-work shone, its green enamel gleamed and painted on its side was a pony's head and the words: Haxton Pony Club.

It stopped smoothly and a woman sprang down from the cabin looking as expensive and newly painted as the box itself.

"Hi-i-i," she called. "Wonderful to be here! We're all absolutely dying to meet you. Wonderful day!"

When the ponies were led out of the box

they, too, were super-bright. The two greys, a bay and a skewbald were all fully clipped out, rugged and bandaged for the journey in vivid yellows and reds. Their tack was clearly the best.

The two boys who had led out the grey ponies, a red-headed girl who had led out the bay and a pale girl who had the skewbald, all looked as if they had stepped out of advertisements for riding clothes in a pony magazine.

"Hi," they called waving vaguely in the direction of the Tarent team. "Hi."

But they didn't really see Sally or Thalia or Simon.

"Is there a cup?" one of the boys asked Simon. "We couldn't find out and one does like to know what one is riding for."

Two slinky cars purred into the yard. The doors opened and Haxton parents filled the yard with noise.

"My dad would get on with them," said Simon. "They could all shout together."

"I'm going to get Tarquin," Thalia announced, seeing Mrs Blair and Martine hurrying across the yard towards them, and she turned her back on the fuss and faffing of the Haxton team.

Although Sally and Verity hung about a little longer the Haxton team did not seem to need any welcoming. Once mounted on their hard, fit ponies they only wanted to get started.

"Mummy, where can we ride them in?"

"Darling, I just do not know. Oh, here's Tilly Blair. She's the one to ask. Hi-i-i! Wonderful to be here. We're all so excited. Now could you tell us . . ."

Sally and Thalia rode down to the field beyond the dressage arena.

"Snobs," said Thalia in disgust.

"They look to me," said Sally, "as if they are going to be brilliant riders as well."

The two Haxton boys rode first in the dressage test. They each performed smooth, correct tests and rode out of the arena looking pleased with themselves.

Thalia was next. Sally watched in dismay as Tarquin refused to stand still while Thalia saluted the judge and then scorched his way through the test – trotting when he should have been walking, cantering when he should have been trotting and where he should have been cantering bursting into a full-out gallop.

Sally was next. She walked Willow into the arena, with the test perfectly clear in her mind, feeling her pony obedient and supple, paying attention to her. She stopped in front of the judge's Land Rover, felt Willow stand four-square, head balanced, ears listening.

Remember to smile, Sally thought as she took her reins into one hand. Her hand was bare when she should have been wearing gloves! Sally's heart thumped in her throat. Mrs Blair had told them so often that they must wear gloves for the dressage test and she had forgotten them.

Panic filled her. Was she eliminated for not wearing gloves? Should she ride out of the arena or should she go on with the test? For moments she sat on Willow, her mind totally blank, not knowing what to do next.

Then she turned Willow and rode to the end of the arena. She stopped, having no idea where to go next. Sally could think of nothing except the terrible fact that she was not wearing gloves and everyone was staring at her. After minutes of muddled riding she found herself back in front of the judge's Land Rover. In an embarrassed attempt to hide her gloveless hands she urged Willow straight out of the arena.

"What went wrong?" yelled Thalia. "You mucked it up! I thought you knew it?"

"I do," muttered Sally, biting her bottom lip to stop herself crying; knowing that she would be eliminated.

It was another disaster in a day when everything went wrong for the Tarent team.

Although they had all walked the cross-country course with Martine, Thalia lost her way. She missed out a bank and was eliminated for taking the wrong course. Simon came off at the ditch and did not complete the course.

After her elimination in the dressage Sally was allowed to go on taking part without competing. She rode Willow over brush fences, barrels, ditches, a wall with an enormous drop, log piles and a bench, all obstacles that Willow had not jumped before. She had two refusals which were both her fault, about six grabs at Willow's mane and a total collapse on to Willow's neck when she landed after the drop.

Only Buster took his rider round successfully, losing time points but finishing safely at his solid canter.

In the showjumping in the afternoon Tarquin cleared all the jumps in high, soaring leaps with Thalia crouched over his withers like a jockey. At every jump Sally was left behind. She clung on to Willow's mane as if she could not jump at all. But she did not care. She only wanted to stay in the saddle. She had given up.

Simon had three refusals at the first jump and was eliminated.

"Zodiac would have jumped that," said Thalia. "I think Simon stopped him."

The Haxton team seemed to Sally to have no faults at all. They had all had good scores over the cross-country. In the showjumping their well-schooled ponies jumped perfectly controlled rounds and they rode out again to the applause of cheering relatives.

"Jolly well done! Well jumped! Good show," cried their parents in loud empty voices.

Mrs Blair presented the rosettes to the Haxton team, thanked them for coming and added that she was sorry the Tarent team had not been able to offer them a little more competition.

Sally heard Mrs Blair's voice without listening to it. She only wanted to go home, to be sitting at the kitchen fire with Meg and Misty beside her.

Mrs Lorimer, Em, Jamie and Narg packed up and drove away. The Haxton team boxed their ponies and were driven away, shouting, "Bye-e-e-e, Bye-e-e-e," their farewells streaming behind them in loud banners of noise.

"Better find Martine," said Thalia in a flat, defeated voice.

Sally nodded and they walked their ponies across towards the horsebox.

"You've to put your ponies in the loose-boxes they were in this morning," Verity shouted running across the yard. "Mum wants to have a word with us," and Verity grasped her throat in both hands and twisted her face into mock strangulation.

"Not surprising," said Charlotte walking

past with her mother. "Considering the team she chose."

Thalia sprang round ready to tell Charlotte what she thought of her but could find nothing to say. It had been a dismal downer of a day.

As Sally took off Willow's tack, a woman she didn't know looked in over the half-door.

"You're the girl from Kestrels, aren't you?" she asked. "I've been trying to speak to your mother all day but I kept missing her."

"She's gone home," said Sally, wanting the woman to go away.

"Drat it! Perhaps you can help. I live at Fintry Bay and we're being plagued by this stray dog. A sort of white greyhound. Great brute of a thing. And now it's started to attack children. We've been in contact with the dog warden, of course. But so far he hasn't managed to catch it. Someone suggested it might be hiding out around Kestrels. Have you seen it?"

Sally stared at the woman; at her stupid doughy face painted like a clown's; her white, blue-tinted hair; the lumps of metal hanging down from holes in her ears and her scarlet nails gripping the loosebox door.

"What do you mean, dangerous? She's not dangerous. She's beautiful. She's the most beautiful dog I've ever seen."

"So you have seen it? It's been annoying you as well? No one's safe with a mad dog like that on the loose. I shall let the warden know that it's been hanging around Kestrels."

Sally stood in the tack room with Thalia, Verity and Simon while Mrs Blair told them what she thought of their performance.

"You would think," she said, "that you had done no schooling, no showjumping, had never jumped a cross-country obstacle in your life. Simon and Thalia, your ponies were totally out of control. I was ashamed of you. There may be some excuse for Simon but none for you, Thalia. You still seem to think it is clever to show off on a pony that could break your neck, going on the way Tarquin does. I had hoped that being in the team would give you a more responsible attitude but there was no sign of it today."

"Yes, but . . ." Thalia began. Mrs Blair totally ignored her.

"And Sally, what went wrong with you? It wasn't Willow, it was you. I thought that you at least would have learnt the dressage test."

But Sally could only think about the silver-white hound. She just could not believe it might be dangerous. She remembered the dog's calm, gentle face and beautiful eyes. Before Sally could believe the ugly rumours she would have to find out more about what had actually happened. Sally thought the woman had looked as if she would call out a spider warden if she found the tiniest spider in her bath. She wished desperately that she had not told the woman that she had seen the hound.

"So I shall see you all next Saturday as usual. Only two weeks until the Event. Though it seems to me there is no point in going on if you can't do better than this."

Martine drove them home to Kestrels in silence. Even Thalia had nothing to say.

They settled their ponies and Thalia went straight home to Narg. Sally walked slowly home to Kestrels, searching the undergrowth for any sign of the white hound. She opened the door, walked into the bright kitchen and knew instantly that something was wrong.

Meg was lying in front of the fire, stretched out as flat and as empty as an old coat that had been left lying there.

"Meg!" cried Sally.

"She's all right," said Mrs Lorimer, speaking too quickly, too anxiously; letting Sally know that Meg was not all right.

"She had another heart attack this afternoon. Dad got the vet and he's increased her pills. He says she'll be all right. We've to let her take it easy for the next few days."

"She is going to get better?" demanded Sally. "She is, isn't she?"

But no one answered her.

"The vet's done everything he can," said Mr Lorimer. "But we've got to remember that she's an old dog."

Chapter Six

The vet came back on Monday evening.

"Just to check up on her," he said as he crouched down to speak to Meg.

Sally stood watching, her hands clenched. It was as if she was trapped in a tunnel; at one end Meg and the vet, at the other end herself. There was nobody else in the whole world; only herself standing spellbound as the vet took out his stethoscope and listened to the beat of Meg's heart. Sally watched his face, intent on listening to this all-important heartbeat that only he could hear.

At last he stood up.

"That's OK," he said. "She's holding

her own. I'll give her another injection."

But to Sally it was nothing like enough.
She wanted the vet to say that Meg was
completely better; was her young self
again.

"Call me if you need me. I'm on the
bleep," the vet told them. "Anyway, I'll
drop in again on Friday. Not sure what
time but I'll fit you in."

Friday was a school holiday.

"Let's work hard," said Thalia, riding
Tarquin down to the shore.

"Yes," said Sally. The shame of doing
so badly against the Haxton team still
shadowed her mind.

For the next half hour they concentrated
on their riding. They made their ponies
walk out with long, balanced strides; circled
at a sitting trot and cantered at a steady,
smooth pace.

"Think Tarquin's had enough," shouted
Thalia and Sally agreed, slowing Willow to
a walk as she clapped her hard, fit neck
and told her she was the best pony in
Tarentshire.

"Let's have a jump," said Thalia.

"The field is pure bog," said Sally, remembering with a cold clutch in her stomach how badly she had been left behind when she had jumped on Saturday. "We'd only churn it up more."

"One go each won't make any difference." Thalia was already turning Tarquin towards Kestrels.

They rode across the ponies' field to where the jumps were standing, abandoned for the winter.

"Hold his reins and I'll sort them out a bit," said Thalia, jumping down from Tarquin.

Sally sat watching as Thalia struggled to set up four jumps in the muddy field. She did not want to jump. She felt cold and nervous, wanting to make up excuses about why she couldn't jump.

Don't start that again, warned the voice in her head. You are in the Pony Club team now. Of course you want to jump.

"There," said Thalia. "How's that? Those four?"

Sally eyed the motley collection of poles,

boxes and oil drums that Thalia had set up. They seemed so high that no one in their right mind would think of jumping them.

She opened her mouth to say that she wasn't going to jump; that it was too muddy; that Willow might slip. Then she saw Thalia watching her with a fixed stare and heard herself saying, "I'll go first."

Tight and cold, Sally rode Willow in a circle and let her canter on at the first jump.

Willow pricked her ears and, timing the jump perfectly, she popped over it. Sally sat neat and still, going with her pony. She landed securely balanced, ready to ride on at the next jump. Her fear had vanished. Totally, completely, as if it had never been.

For I can jump now, Sally thought. Even if I do make mistakes and get mixed up, it doesn't matter, I can jump. She rode back to Thalia grinning broadly, because she knew now and nothing could change it.

Normally Thalia would have gathered up Tarquin's reins and sent him galloping wildly over the jumps, but today she didn't. She circled Tarquin at a trot, then at a slow canter. She halted him, then rode forward and halted again. Then she trotted him in a circle, only letting him canter as they rode at the first jump.

After the barrels, when normally Tarquin would have been charging madly on, more or less out of control, Thalia turned him away from the jumps and, trotting in circles, she settled him before they cleared the last two jumps.

"I've changed," Thalia announced, walking on a loose rein over to Sally. "Not for cross-country. If in doubt kick them on. That's what Princess Anne said and she's right. But, I suppose, for showjumping he is a bit mad."

"They've all been telling you that for months!"

"It was Charlotte who did it. I could hardly stop Tarquin after the show-jumping against the Haxton lot. We almost galloped straight into Charlotte and her mother and she says in her great, loud, spotty voice, 'Don't mind us. Out of control as usual, are we?' and then she laughed. You know the way she does. So

I thought ... Perhaps I should ... So that's why."

By lunchtime the vet still hadn't been to see Meg. When she had finished her lunch Sally sat down beside Meg where she lay on her rug in front of the fire.

"You're a good, dear Meg," she said. "When Mr Cheever comes this afternoon he'll say you're a lot better, I know he will."

Meg lifted her head and thumped the rug with her tail but she didn't really want to be bothered with anyone. Not even Sally. She let her head drop back on to the rug and in seconds she was asleep again, the sound of her noisy breathing filling the kitchen.

"Try not to upset yourself too much," said her mother. "She's still eating well and poddling about the garden when she feels like it. Why don't you take Misty for a walk? She hasn't had a decent walk for days."

Sally took Misty down to the sands and threw sticks for her. Barking at her absolute loudest, Misty raced after the sticks, leaping and jumping in furious tornadoes of white and grey hair.

But Sally couldn't stop wondering if the vet had been or if he might be at Kestrels at that very moment. She whistled Misty and began to walk home. As she went along her eyes searched Kestrels' grounds for any sign of the white hound, but there was only the autumn tangle of leaves, dying grasses and dense bushes. No white shape was waiting in the undergrowth or racing over the muddied lawns and when she got home the vet still hadn't been.

Thalia and Sally rode in the afternoon and then cleaned tack and groomed.

"Perhaps it's a different dog that frightened the children," suggested Thalia as she worked on Tarquin's mane. "Maybe the men took their dog away with them."

"No," Sally shouted in reply as she scrubbed at Willow's muddied fetlocks. "They'd gone the last time I saw the dog. Left her behind. Who's feeding her now? Who's looking after her?"

Thalia had no answers and Sally did

not know what else she could do to find the dog. She had left her unicorn at her window, so it would be there if the hound came to Kestrels. Sally knew that everyone else would think it was a silly nonsense but it hadn't stopped her standing the unicorn securely on the windowsill and leaving it there all the time.

Mr Lorimer had come back from his library; Emma and Ben had come home from school and there was still no vet. They all ate their supper with ears alert for the vet's car but it wasn't until Ben and Sally had finished washing up and Jamie had spread out his train set for a last ten minutes before he went to bed that there was a knock on the door.

Emma ran to open it with Sally close behind her.

A small, dark-haired man in a tweed cap, waxed jacket and wellington boots stood there.

"Good evening," he said, showing false teeth as he smiled at them. "Is your dad in?"

"Evening," said Mr Lorimer coming to the door. "Can I help you?"

"I'm Hugh Brown, Dog Warden," and he took a plastic card from his pocket and flickered it in front of Mr Lorimer. "Could I have a few words with you about a white greyhound? I believe it's been seen round here."

"In you come," said Mr Lorimer and Hugh Brown came into the kitchen to perch on the edge of a chair. Sally stared at him, hating everything about him. How dare he come into her house, hunting down the white hound? Sally knew what the dog warden would do if he caught the hound. He would kill her.

"It seems to have been abandoned. Nasty-natured beast. Went for a little boy in Fintry."

"You mean it bit him?" asked Mr Lorimer.

"Not exactly. A near thing. Lucky his mum was there to chase the dog off or we'd have had a TV interview on our hands. Once you get a dog who's a loner like this one, no saying what they'll do next."

Sally stood with her back to the door scowling at the dog warden.

"The white hound's not a bit like that," she said. "She's a beautiful dog. She would never hurt anyone!"

"Ah," said the dog warden. "So you've seen her? Prowling round your grounds?"

Sally blushed scarlet.

"No!" she said. "Of course I haven't seen her. She's never been here."

"Didn't you see a white dog from your bedroom window?" asked her mother. "You told us about it. Perhaps the same dog?"

"That wasn't the white hound . . ." began Sally and then stopped, realising that the more she said the worse she made things.

"I must warn you not to go near the dog. She could be dangerous. If you see her, phone the police and they'll contact me."

Mr Lorimer said they all understood and they'd let the warden know if there was any sign of the dog.

Never, thought Sally. I'd never phone

the police. Sally knew that some dogs could be dangerous. She had read about it in the papers. Seen the horrific photographs of children with torn faces. She was certain that the hound wasn't like that. Not vicious. Abandoned and afraid, but not vicious. Sally could not believe that such a calm, gentle dog could be dangerous.

"Would it be all right if I have a look round your grounds tomorrow?" asked the dog warden. Mr Lorimer said it would.

The vet arrived minutes after the dog warden left. He was in a hurry, going straight to Meg, uncoiling his stethoscope as he went. But when he listened to Meg's heart he slowed down, listening carefully, giving her his full attention.

All the Lorimers waited tensely until he stood up.

"Is she eating?" he asked. "No trouble with her bowels?"

"She's fine," said Mrs Lorimer. "Drinking more than she used to and doesn't want to move much. Out for a few minutes and then back in to lie down again."

"Right," said the vet. "I don't like the sound of her heart tonight. Thought it might have steadied up a bit by now. There is one thing we could try. Bit of a gamble. Might work, might not. It boosts the whole system. It depends how strong the dog is whether they can pull through on it or not. If it works for them, things are looking good."

"Sounds rather desperate," said Mr Lorimer.

"It is," said the vet. "But I think in Meg's case we are going to have to consider it. I'll come back tomorrow, have another listen and we can make the decision then."

The vet gave Meg an injection, then crouched down and spoke to her. He ran his hand gently over her head, telling her she was a brave old lady, while Meg regarded him calmly from deep-brown eyes.

Sally took Meg out before she went to bed. She steadied her down the step and waited while Meg sniffed about the grass.

On their way back into the house Meg sat down on the doorstep. Sally stopped beside her. She couldn't bear to think that Meg was going to die.

Sally knelt beside Meg and took her head in both her hands.

"Listen," she said, speaking directly to Meg. "You are not going to die. You are going to get better."

Chapter Seven

"Why couldn't you all have ridden like that last week?" demanded Mrs Baird looking round at her team as they stood holding their ponies and listening to her. They had just spent the afternoon being instructed by Martine as they repeated the cross-country and showjumping courses that they had ridden over last weekend against the Haxton team.

"I forgot my gloves," said Sally. "Then everything else went wrong."

"They were all so posh," said Thalia. "All looking down their noses at us."

"You knew they were the best," Verity said accusingly. "You knew how good they were before you invited them."

Mrs Blair laughed. "Perhaps I did," she admitted. "It let you know what you'll be up against. They will be there on Saturday so that gives you the chance to get your own back."

"We will," stated Thalia.

Martine had been very pleased by the way Tarquin had calmed down when he was showjumping. Thalia had her praise stored in her mind. She would listen to it properly when she was alone.

"Now," said Mrs Blair checking the lists in her hand. "I've spoken to all your parents. They are all coming. We will need first-class support. On Saturday morning you will all be here at eight o'clock. Martine is bringing Sally and Thalia and their ponies. Verity is here and Simon, your father is bringing you and Zodiac in your trailer and you can box her here. You are sure that Zodiac will be fully shod for the Event?"

"She will," said Simon, looking down at the ground.

Simon had arrived riding Clover, telling

them that Zodiac had cast a shoe and couldn't be ridden until the blacksmith had been. Simon had not jumped the cross-country obstacles, saying that Clover was not fit.

Sally had been delighted to see Clover again. She was looking sleek and contented and years younger than when she had been a riding-school pony at Miss Meek's. Simon, too, looked as if he was enjoying riding her. Sally remembered how white and strained Simon had looked when he had led Zodiac away from the cross-country. Although he had ridden in the showjumping phase he had had three refusals at the first jump and he had not remounted in the cross-country.

Stop it! Sally told herself. You're getting as bad as Charlotte, and she turned her attention back to Mrs Blair just in time to hear Mrs Blair telling her that she was to pin a clean pair of gloves on to her jacket sleeve.

"If you need help, let me know," said Martine as they unloaded Willow and Tarquin in Kestrels' yard. "I shall phone you on Friday evening to rouse you on. Keep up the good work with Tarquin. I'm expecting an A+ dressage test. And Sally, remember to look up, look over the jump, not at it."

Now that she was home Sally only wanted to find out how Meg was. She took Willow's tack off, put the water bucket into her box and, tossing in an armful of hay, she told Thalia that she would be back in a minute.

Glimpsed through the lighted kitchen window Meg lay flattened on the hearth rug, her breathing lifting her whole body. Misty and Mrs Lorimer were busy at the cooker.

"How is she?" Sally cried, dashing into the kitchen.

Her mother turned round quickly, her finger to her lips. Misty bounded to meet her but Meg didn't move.

"Shh! Don't disturb her. We had to phone the vet. She had another turn."

"What did he say?" demanded Sally urgently, speaking from a far, cold place, her voice frozen to a whisper.

"He's changed her pills to the ones he told us about. Although there is a risk, at least they'll give her a chance."

Sally's eyes filled with tears. She wanted her mother to comfort her but Mrs Lorimer, searching in her apron for her handkerchief, was crying herself.

"He says we've not to give up hope because there is a good chance that she'll pull through."

Sally stood looking down at Meg, listening to the gasp and drag of her breathing.

"Don't disturb her," Mrs Lorimer warned again. "The more she sleeps the better. We've to keep her as quiet as possible. Only fish or chicken and well-boiled brown rice. It will be a week before we'll know whether she can cope with the pills."

Sally turned away and went back to Willow. She threw her arms round her pony's neck and buried her face in Willow's mane.

"Is it Meg?" asked Thalia, standing hesitantly in the doorway.

"She's had another heart attack," mumbled Sally.

"You mean she's not dead?" cried Thalia. "Well, that's good. If she's not dead then there's lots that we can do for her."

Sally explained what the vet had said.

"That means we have the whole of medical science working for us! What we've got to do is help Meg. We've got to think of her as she will be – quite completely better. Running and barking and chasing Misty. That's what Narg always does. I'll tell her to think about Meg. You mustn't think for the least second that she might not get better. See her well and happy again."

Sally lifted her head, scrubbed at her eyes with a bit of paper handkerchief and pushed her hair back behind her ears.

"Imagine her well all the time," insisted Thalia.

Sally pictured Meg coming into the loosebox, sitting down to wait for her as she had done so many times, her bright eyes gleaming through her shaggy hair and her black nose glistening as Willow blew through her nostrils welcoming Meg. As Sally walked back home, leaving Willow with a deep straw bed and a full haynet, she imagined Meg running in front of her, barking impatiently.

"Did anyone tell Sally about the meat?" Em asked as they were finishing their meal.

"What meat?" Sally asked.

"Obviously not," said her father. "The dog warden came back while you were at Mrs Blair's. He'd a look round and thinks the white dog may have been sleeping in the summerhouse. There's an old rug there and it's covered with white hairs. He's left some drugged meat near the rug, hoping the dog will come back tonight, eat it, fall asleep, and if so it should still be there in the morning when he comes to check up. No one is to go near the summerhouse."

Guilt flooded over Sally – that the white hound had been living at Kestrels and she hadn't known; fury that the dog warden had been to Kestrels, mixed with rage that he should have dared to leave drugged meat in their summerhouse.

"It might be drugged meat for a hound," exclaimed Sally, her voice loud and shouting, not at all a supper table voice. "But what about a cat or a fox? It would be poison for them."

"He promised us that it was not poisoned. It will only make any animal unconscious."

"If the dog is as dangerous as he says it is we must help him to catch it," said Mrs Lorimer. "You can't have dogs going around attacking children. Be sensible, Sally."

Sally gazed despairingly at her parents. She had tried to explain to them that she had seen the hound; that it was quiet and gentle and beautiful; that she understood that stray dogs could be dangerous but that the hound was not. She knew that once her parents saw the hound they would understand. But she could not make them listen to her.

Mrs Lorimer gave Meg her pills. She took them without any fuss, then pulled herself stiffly to her feet and walked the few steps to her bowl. She stood for a minute until she got her balance, then she lowered her head to lap the water. When she had finished she turned without looking at any of them and slowly reached her rug again. Her legs gave way and she collapsed. In seconds she was asleep again.

Sally caught the quick look that passed between her mother and father and instantly she knew what they were thinking – that it would be the kindest thing to have Meg put down.

"We have all to think of her as being well again. Thalia says that's what her narg does. You must not feel sorry for her but all the time imagine she's better."

To Sally's surprise no one argued with her. Even Jamie scrunged up his face and said he could see Meg eating sweets he had given her.

Sally waited until all her family had settled to their evening occupations – Ben to his books, Emma to her homework, her father to doze over the telly and her mother to read Jamie his bedtime story.

Sally left the living room quietly. In the kitchen she pulled on her anorak, found a plastic bag in the drawer and, picking up the torch from its place on the dresser, she silently opened the door. She crept through, closed it and listened. She had escaped. Misty had not heard her.

Sally followed the bobbing, yellow light of her torch across the grass, through the autumn tangle of bushes and shrubs until she saw the summerhouse and beyond it the moonlit glitter of the black, quicksilver sea.

Sally stood still, swinging her torch in wide swathes of yellow light. Nothing moved. There was no sign of the white hound. Sally shivered, suddenly wishing that she had brought Misty with her or gone for Thalia. But she knew that she would never find the white hound if there was someone else with her. She had to wait in the summerhouse by herself.

The dog warden had put the meat on the floor, close to the old blanket that had been left lying there. Sally put her hand into the plastic bag, picked up the meat, then pulled the bag over it. She had picked it up without touching it. No matter what the dog warden had said Sally was sure it was poisoned.

She sat down on the window seat, folded her arms and, staring out into the dark, moon-gleaming gardens, she waited for the hound to come.

First of all Sally concentrated on Meg, seeing her well again, then she rode Willow through the dressage test. Her head nodded and her eyes closed.

Willow and Tarquin had wings. Thalia and Sally raced them over sea the colour of amethysts and over banks of white cloud. As they rode someone was watching them.

Sally's eyelids twitched. She woke from her dream, realising that she had been asleep. Yet part of the dream was real. There was someone watching her. Cautiously, she opened her eyes. Framed in the doorway of the summerhouse stood the white hound.

For a second Sally felt her skin creep,

her spine tighten. The hound seemed to have come from a dark world of enchanted fairy tales. Then Sally moved slightly and the dog walked towards her, hardly disturbing the darkness. Her long, fine legs, arched neck and high, lean body moved in silence.

She came right up to Sally, placed a knuckled paw on her knee and laid her almost weightless head in Sally's lap. She stood perfectly still, gazing up at Sally with loyalty and love.

Chapter Eight

Sally held her breath, terrified to move in case she should frighten the hound, but she did not seem to be at all afraid. She gazed up at Sally through her strange, blue-white eyes. Only the tip of her sickle tail moved from side to side.

Gradually Sally ran her hand down the hound's neck and along the knotted ridge of her spine. Sally felt her ribs stretching through her harsh skin and realised how thin she was, even for a greyhound.

"Poor dog," she whispered. "Did those men leave you behind? But you're my dog now. I'm going to keep you. I don't care what anyone says – you're going to stay with us. You need a name. That will make you belong to us."

Sally thought of dog names. It had to be the right name. She waited for it to come into her mind.

"Fenella," she said at last. "I shall call you Fen.

The hound, who had been listening intently, pawed at Sally's knee and pushed at her elbow with her long muzzle.

"That's it: Fen.

"Now, stay with me," Sally said standing up slowly, terrified that the hound might race away and vanish into the dark. There was no handful of beardie hair to grasp. Nothing to hold on to.

Step by step, Sally set off along the path to Kestrels and Fen moved gracefully at her side, showing no signs of wanting to leave her.

As the lighted windows of Kestrels came into sight, Sally hesitated, wondering what her family would say. Would her mother want another dog, especially when the dog warden thought she might be dangerous? Would she be all right with

Meg – for nothing must be allowed to disturb Meg.

Fen looked up questioningly, a front paw lifted.

"Of course they'll want you," Sally told her. "Of course they will." She marched on into the house.

"Where on earth did you find her?" demanded her father.

"She is some size," said her mother.

"But beautiful!" exclaimed Em, coming to stroke her.

Fen paid no attention to anyone, not even to Misty who was bounding and bouffing just out of Fen's reach. The hound stood by Sally's side gazing mildly around the kitchen. She saw Meg lying in front of the fire and walked across to her. Fen looked down and Meg startled awake. She lifted her head up and Fen stretched her neck out so that their noses almost touched. There was a moment of silence, then Meg gave a gusty sigh and lay down again, putting her head carefully on the rug, not letting it fall back because she was too exhausted to do anything else.

And in that moment Sally was filled with a certainty that Meg would get better.

"She's going to be all right," Sally began, turning to her family, but no one was paying any attention to her.

Mrs Lorimer was warning Jamie not to go too close to the hound, her father was looking up the dog warden's telephone number, while Emma was opening a tin of dog food.

"She's ours," Sally said to her father. "She belongs to me. I've named her Fen, so we must keep her. Please don't phone the dog warden. He doesn't need to know I found her. We can keep her and just not tell him."

"No, Sally. Of course we must let him know," said Mr Lorimer as he phoned the dog warden and left a message.

"But you won't let him take her away?"

"We'll see what he has to say," stated Mr Lorimer. "If he still thinks she is dangerous she will have to go."

"Honestly, she doesn't look dangerous to me," said Ben, stroking Fen. "She's a super dog. I vote we keep her."

Fen had eaten the food that Em had given to her, had a drink and was lying by the table watching them all through gentle eyes. Her long, spilliken, ivory legs were sprawled out on the carpet, her knuckled paws folded over, completely ignoring Misty who was mithering about her.

"She's certainly made herself at home," said Mr Lorimer.

"That's because she is at home," said Sally. "Kestrels is her home."

"She does seem a nice dog," admitted Mr Lorimer. "Perhaps she wouldn't be any trouble."

Nice! thought Sally. How could her father possibly see Fen as "nice"? She was a hound from King Arthur's court who had ridden out with the knights, or a hound from an Egyptian temple led out by the priests in procession behind the god king.

"We MUST keep her," she said.

"Don't upset yourself tonight," said her mother. "Shouldn't think there's any chance of the dog warden coming out now. Much too late."

Sally supposed not. Reluctantly she got out her homework and tried to do her sentences.

The knock on the door made them all jump. No one had heard a car.

"Hide her!" cried Sally desperately, sure it must be the dog warden.

"Don't be silly," warned her mother as Mr Lorimer brought the dog warden into the kitchen.

"That's her all right," said the warden, seeing the hound at once in spite of Sally's efforts to stand in front of Fen and hide her. "Any trouble? I'll take her away with me."

"No!" cried Sally desperately. "She is my dog. You can't have her!"

The warden took a leather collar from his pocket and buckled it round the white hound's neck.

"Seems quiet enough now," he said.

"Of course she is," cried Sally, and she flung her arms round Fen trying to pull her away from the warden.

"Let's keep her," pleaded Em.

"You know what Sally will be like if we don't," said Ben. "Tears and torment for weeks."

The warden let the hound go and Sally pulled her close to her side.

Mrs Lorimer looked at Mr Lorimer lifting her eyebrows and Mr Lorimer looked at the dog warden who pushed his hand through his hair.

"There seems to have been only one incident involving a child," he admitted. "I tracked down the parents this afternoon. Their boy had a packet of crisps and I reckon he was teasing the dog. Offering her a crisp and then snatching it away from her, and all she did was bark at him. Then the boy blew up the crisp packet and burst it in her face. She bolted, knocked the boy over and all the rumours grew from that."

"Would it be all right if we kept her?" said Mrs Lorimer. "I can't bear to think of her being put down."

"Oh, thank you! Thank you!" cried Sally in delight.

"Not easy for me either," said the dog warden and he paused. "Still, you seem a family that's used to dogs. I'll chance it. Leave her with you for a week. Any sign of bad temper you must let me know at once and I'll be out for her."

"Oh, but you won't need to come back," Sally assured him. "We'll look after her for ever."

"I'll be round next Saturday."

"That's the one-day-event," said Mrs Lorimer. "We may all be out."

"Evening, then," said the dog warden and took forms out of his inside pocket for Mr Lorimer to sign.

Sally went quietly to bed, not saying goodnight to anyone. Fen walked at her heels and if her mother saw her she said nothing.

Fen curled up on the mat by Sally's bed, her long muzzle tucked into the crook of her leg. Sitting up in bed Sally looked from the tiny shape of the unicorn silhouetted against the sky to the ivory hound, sleeping as peacefully as if she had lived with the Lorimers all her life.

In a week, in only seven short days, the dog warden would be back; they would know if the pills were working for Meg and it would be the one-day-event. Be now. Be over. A day to be remembered. Sally wrapped her arms round herself, shivering with a mixture of delight and fear. Her head touched her pillow and she slept.

Thalia was umbridged that Sally had not phoned her when she found Fen.

"You might have needed me. I could have let his tyres down to stop him taking Fen away!"

The vet came to see Meg on Wednesday.

"He's pleased with her," Mrs Lorimer told Sally when she came in from school.

As if she knew what they were saying Met sat up, wagging her tail, and crossed the room to Sally.

"You are a bit better," cried Sally dropping on her knees to stroke Meg, afraid to say more just in case. "Dear dog, dear, dear Meg."

Misty came leaping and bounding about

them but Fen waited quietly by Meg's side, making sure that Misty didn't knock her over.

"The vet can't be certain until the end of the week, but the pills do seem to be agreeing with her," her mother said as Meg snuffled her face into Sally's anorak pocket, smelling a bit of chocolate that Sally had forgotten about. When she couldn't reach it Meg sat down and barked her command that Sally should give her the chocolate immediately. Gobbling it up Meg seemed almost her old self again.

The Friday before the one-day-event was the longest, slowest school day that Sally and Thalia had ever known, but when they got home to Kestrels the evening vanished in the stamp of a pony's hoof.

Straight after school they rode their ponies down to the shore and schooled them, each thinking the same thing – that the next time they rode, it would be in the one-day-event.

Thalia was sleeping at Kestrels, so when they had finished eating Mrs Lorimer's home-made pie and chips they went out to the stables and groomed until their arms ached and their ponies shone.

"Now for the tack," said Thalia, refusing to give in to Sally's suggestion that they should have a drink of juice before they started.

Mrs Lorimer made them go to bed early.

"If you have to be up at five, you must get some sleep," she insisted. "Off you go."

They sat up in bed taking it in turns to go over the dressage test, pushing one of Sally's china ponies round the duvet. Their riding clothes, washed and ironed by Mrs Lorimer and Narg, hung outside the wardrobe. A pair of yellow string gloves was pinned to the sleeve of Sally's jacket and Thalia's new hat hung from its own hook on the back of the door. Mr Lorimer had polished their boots and their shine would have passed any sergeant major's examination.

"Tomorrow," said Sally. "Everything is waiting for tomorrow. Willow and

Tarquin and all the other ponies and their riders."

"Clean tack and clean clothes," said Thalia. "Especially my hat."

"Petrol in the horseboxes. Cross-country obstacles."

"Martine and Mrs Blair wanting us to do well," said Thalia. "The Tarent team sure they are going to win."

"And me," said Sally. "Me who could hardly ride at all a few months ago." And the thought of tomorrow swept over Sally like the sea.

Chapter Nine

Martine drove the horsebox into the parking area of Leighton Hall. Ponies were being unloaded, bandages taken off and girths checked while children and parents shouted at each other in loud, excited voices. Peering from the cabin window Sally and Thalia could see nothing but bustle and action and when they jumped out they could feel the excitement in the air.

It's all real, Sally thought. I am here to ride in a one-day-event. It's not a pony book I'm reading. It is really going to happen!

Verity and Simon, who had come in

their parents' cars, came running across to them.

"Dad's been bawling his head off," said Simon. "Thinks I'm not going to have enough time to ride Zodiac in."

"Well, he can stop worrying now. We have arrived," said Martine, and she took them across to the edge of the parking area. "This will give you an idea of where you are."

From a rise in the ground they could see the one-day-event spread out before them. There was the practice area, a rough field where several ponies were being ridden in; the newly mown dressage area with brightly painted white letters set correctly round its edges; next to it the roped-in showjumping ring and, curving out of sight between a broad river and a clump of lime trees, was the beginning of the cross-country course. They could see the first two jumps – rustic poles and a brush jump. Red flag markers on the right of the obstacles and white flag markers on the left, hung limply in the moist air.

"Remember," said Martine. "You must

ride between the flags or you'll be eliminated."

"But we will be walking round the cross-country, won't we?" asked Simon.

Sally, hearing the strain in his voice, looked round at Simon. His face was drawn and tense, his lips closed into a tight line and his eyebrows gathered in. He looked every bit as nervous as he had done before Tarent Show.

"With me to guide you every hoof print of the way," Martine assured him.

Mrs Blair came bustling towards them.

"Time you were all mounted," she said, organising them back to the horsebox. "Now I only expect one thing – that you all do your best. Sally, you've got your gloves? Thalia, we do not want any rodeo displays."

Martine slipped down to the back of the horsebox and, speaking calmly to the ponies, she began to untie their halter ropes and hand them to their riders.

Verity led Buster out. Zodiac plunged down the ramp almost dragging Simon off his feet. Sally took Willow and Thalia shouted at Tarquin, yanked at his halter rope, and managed to keep him to a walk as he clattered out of the box.

Glancing back into the gaping black cave of the horsebox, Sally thought she saw something moving. From the ledge at the very back of the box which was piled with blankets and rugs, a long, white, hound's face looked out at them. Two slender bony legs pushed through beneath the face and Fen flowed down from between the blankets.

"Ye gods!" cried Martine, seeing Fen at the same time as Sally. "How on earth did she get here?"

Knowing she had done wrong Fen slunk out of the box and crouched down close to Sally.

Mrs Blair was not amused.

"Put her in the cabin and leave her there until your parents arrive," she told Sally. "They can do what they like with her. You are about to ride a dressage test."

Shut in the cabin of the horsebox Fen scrabbled wildly, tearing at the window, trying to open it.

"Leave her alone," Mrs Blair warned Sally, and began to check over her team's riding clothes and their ponies' tack.

All the time Mrs Blair was speaking Fen kept up her furious attempts to escape.

"This is no use," cried Martine in exasperation. "We can't let her go on creating that racket," and she wrenched open the cabin door letting Fen leap to the ground and race to Sally's side.

"When are your parents coming?" demanded Mrs Blair.

"Soon," said Sally, feeling it was all her fault but not quite knowing why. "Perhaps they're searching for Fen."

Mrs Blair phoned Kestrels from her car phone and was told by Ben that his parents, Em and Jamie had left Kestrels about an hour after the horsebox. They hadn't noticed that Fen was missing.

The others rode down to the schooling area while Mrs Blair found a rope lead in the boot of her car and looped it round Fen's neck. But when Sally rode away Fen pulled free from Mrs Blair and charged after Sally.

"Oh, honestly!" shouted Mrs Blair. "Dratted dog! Well, I must see about your entries. You'll need to dismount and come with me to the secretary's caravan."

Holding Fen by the rope and Willow by her reins Sally stood outside the caravan watching the others riding in their ponies and wishing desperately that her parents would arrive.

Mrs Blair came out of the caravan with their numbered tabards and called her team together.

"As you know our team's drawn second-last in the running order. Thalia, you're 13, Sally, 14, Simon, 15 and Verity, 16. That's your order in all phases.

"Lucky you're almost last," Mrs Blair said to Sally. "It should give your parents time to get here and take over the hound."

"And the rest of you," organised Martine, "on you go and wake your ponies up. Some hard schooling. Get them to pay attention to you."

"Be best if you wait by the horsebox. You'll see your family driving in. Now don't worry. I'll come back and we'll sort things out in plenty of time," said Mrs Blair as she hurried off, shouting to Verity to kick Buster on.

Sally found a place where she could see the dressage arena and watch for their car. People passing stared curiously at her. Several adults stopped to ask if they could help and Sally told them that she was all right, just waiting.

One by one she saw ponies leave the practice area, wait for their turn to ride into the arena and, like clockwork toys, each follow exactly the same pattern before they rode out again.

I should be there, Sally thought despairingly. We're going to miss our turn. It's not fair. Not fair. Oh, Fen, it is your fault. You should have stayed at home. But a bit of Sally couldn't help being pleased that Fen had stowed away to be with her.

"Darling," cried Mrs Lorimer running towards her daughter. "How on earth did Fen get here? And why are you by yourself? Shouldn't you be riding?"

"She came with us in the box. I didn't know she was there and she won't behave herself without me. The dressage started ages ago and I should be riding Willow in before it's my turn."

"Right," said Mrs Lorimer, asking no questions. "Let me have Fen."

She took the rope from Sally, and Fen greeted Em and Mr Lorimer with her sharp, tight bark.

Hardly waiting to thank her family, Sally trotted Willow over to the field and started to ride her in.

Willow had been bored being dragged about by her reins, not understanding what was happening. Now she pricked her ears and walked out with a long stride. She trotted and cantered freely when Sally asked her to, changing her paces smoothly. As she rode Sally forgot about the muddle of the morning, the trouble with Fen. She was thinking only of Willow, riding as if she really was part of her pony.

Waiting by the dressage arena Sally watched Thalia ride her test, holding her breath when Tarquin's canter became a pounding gallop.

The judge tooted her horn.

"They're ready for you," said Martine.

Sally took a deep breath and rode into the arena. At the centre she halted Willow, who stood four-square without a movement while Sally dropped her right hand, correct in its yellow glove, to her side, and saluted the judge with a nod of her head.

She had only ridden the complete dressage test once before but now all Sally's hours of schooling stood her in good stead. The different movements fell into place as easily as the correct pieces of a jigsaw being fitted together. Willow's trot took her into the corners of the arena, she turned smartly, changing pace accurately at the correct letter. All Willow's movements were calm and smooth as Sally rode her through the test. In what seemed to Sally no time at all, she had completed the last movement, saluted the judge and was riding out of the arena at a free walk on a loose rein.

"That," said Martine, "was quite something!"

"It just happened," Sally said. "It was all Willow," and she hid her face in Willow's mane to hide her embarrassment at having done so well.

When the results of the dressage were posted in the window of the caravan Sally had the lowest number of penalty points which meant she was first in the dressage phase. Verity was eighth, Thalia thirteenth and Simon fifteenth.

"Fantastic!" cried Thalia. "Absolutely brilliant!"

"Early days," cautioned Mrs Blair.

"Of course," agreed Thalia, "it is the cross-country that really matters."

During the lunch-break they walked the cross-country. After the first two jumps there were three jumps in amongst the trees, then a drop jump with a pole in front of it and a water jump over the river. After that they galloped on over a string of jumps stretching out over the open country.

Sally listened intently to Martine's instructions. She studied the obstacles, thinking how she would tackle them. She had totally forgotten to be afraid.

"It's absolutely super," enthused Thalia. "Tarquin will fly round it."

"One thing about Buster," said Verity, "is that he knows how to look after himself. We won't be first but we'll be safest."

Only Simon knew that the drop jump out of the wood was exactly the same as the jump where he had had his accident.

"It's about an hour before the cross-country starts," said Martine. "Get yourselves organised. Change into your sweaters. You all know your starting time? We'll be watching out for you. Good luck to you all."

Sally was riding Willow in when she suddenly saw Fen racing towards her.

"Where have you been?" Sally cried, seeing Fen's legs, shoulder and head were covered with black gleaming mud. "What's happened to you?"

Fen raced straight up to Sally and gripped the heel of Sally's boot in her jaws. Then she let go of it, ran off for a few strides and stood barking at Sally, obviously wanting Sally to follow her.

"What do you want?" demanded Sally, then stopped in horror. A glint of sun on Fen's muddied head and shoulder showed something that Sally had not noticed before.

Although Fen was not injured the side of her head and down her neck to her shoulder were bright with blood.

Chapter Ten

Sally froze. For a moment of blind panic she could only hear the dog warden's warnings; could only think that Fen had attacked a child.

Fen came running back, gripped Sally's boot again, and tugging wildly she tried to make Sally pay attention to her.

For a second Sally looked round for help, then she realised that whatever had happened she had to find out the truth for herself.

Fen ran in front of Sally, who urged Willow into a gallop to keep up with her. They raced towards the river in the opposite direction to the cross-country.

Fen leapt down from the field to a broad strand of river bank made up of shingle. Rocks set in the smooth flowing river churned it into torrents of foam.

Lying on the shingle, just clear of the rocks and the river, was a little boy who looked about three years old. His face was scraped and bleeding and his fair hair sticky with blood from a gash on his head. For a split second Sally thought that Fan had attacked him, and then she saw the track in the shingle where he had been pulled from the water. She watched Fen grab his coat and try to pull him further away from the river.

Sally leapt down from Willow, remembering that you should never try to move anyone who has had an accident. She turned the child's head on one side and loosened his clothing with fumbling hands. Although he was unconscious he was breathing easily.

Telling Fen to stay, Sally jumped back on to Willow and galloped for help. There was an ambulance at the start of the cross-country. Sally charged through ponies and riders, past spectators and stewards, and reaching the ambulance she shouted for help.

When the ambulance reached the little boy several people who had seen Sally and Fen galloping to the river had come over to find out what was happening. Emma was there with Fen securely held by her rope, as was the child's mother who had been searching everywhere for her son. The ambulance men lifted the child on to a stretcher and with his mother beside him, they drove away.

"We'd gone back to the car for a drink of juice," explained Emma. "Fen had settled down on the back seat. She didn't seem to want to come with us when we were ready to go back to the cross-country, so we left her. The window was a bit open. She must have squeezed through and gone to the river for a drink."

Sally wanted to say it was a good job, for if Fen hadn't found the child he might have drowned. She wanted to tell Em how clever Fen was, dragging the child to safety but her teeth were chattering so much she couldn't speak. She leant against Willow shivering uncontrollably.

"Have you ridden in the cross-country?" Emma asked.

Sally shook her head. She could hardly bring her mind back to thoughts of the cross-country, she was so relieved that Fen had not attacked the little boy.

Thalia came charging up on Tarquin.

"They sent me to find you," she shouted. "Hurry up. It'll be our turn in about twenty minutes. What's wrong? Are you ill?"

Emma explained.

"But she's got to ride!" exclaimed Thalia. "It's for the team. She must."

Somehow Sally forced her rubbery legs to climb back on to Willow and once she was riding again she felt better. The cross-country mattered; the team was real again.

Sally hardly had time to ride Willow in before it was time for the Tarent team to ride. Thalia went first, Sally second, Simon third and Verity last. There were two minutes between each start.

Waiting, Sally saw Thalia go galloping out, clear the rustic poles, gallop on and over the stone wall, swing right and on out of sight into the shelter of the trees.

Sally gathered Willow together, niggling with her heels on her sides and her fingers on the reins.

"We'll do it. We'll do it easily," she told Willow and as she galloped free from the start she was filled with energy and excitement. The cross-country was a challenge, a delight.

With pounding hooves and pricked ears, Willow carried Sally over the first two jumps. She swung round into the softer going of the track between the trees and bounced over a white-painted gate. There was one more jump over a fallen tree trunk before the track sloped downhill.

Sally heard Martine's voice warning them to steady their ponies before they rode downhill and sitting down in the saddle she tightened her hands on Willow's reins and felt her pony's canter change to a trot.

A row of painted barrels stretched across the steep track. Willow goggled suspiciously at them but Sally drove her on and Willow leaped suddenly and sharply into the air to clear them. She touched down and in another few strides they were over the pole in front of the drop and out of the wood.

The water jump was next. Willow took off well before they reached the bank of the river which was churned into deep mud by galloping hooves. Willow leapt in a low arc over the poles set in the middle of the river, to land far out on the other side. The open course spread out before them.

Remembering time faults Sally pushed her pony on and Willow responded willingly. Never before had Sally ridden like this; never before had she known such freedom.

From the corner of her eye she glimpsed red flags on the right side, saw stewards with clip boards, but they were no part of Sally's flying ecstasy. She rode over the short turf, under the high, blue autumn sky as if there were only herself and her pony jumping and galloping in a newly created world.

They reached the furthest point of the course and circled round towards the finish. They rode over wattle fencing, jumped in and out through a sheep pen, over a brush fence and a spread of poles over a ditch. The last fence was a painted wishing well which Willow cleared with a soaring leap and then galloped on through the finish.

"You made it!" yelled Thalia. "How did you get on?"

Sally flung her reins loose and threw her arms round Willow's neck. It was too soon to come back to the world of Thalia and winning. Too soon. She wanted to stay in the bewitched magic world of galloping and jumping.

"Did she have any refusals? Did she stop?"

Sally shook her head and slid down from Willow, clapping her and thanking her.

"Well? What happened? Tell me!"

Thalia was not to be denied.

"I don't know," said Sally. "I think we were clear. But it was super. Absolutely super."

Words weren't enough. She couldn't begin to tell Thalia.

"So was I. Clear. So was I," rejoiced Thalia.

Mrs Blair came hurrying across with sweat rugs, asking questions, telling them to loosen off their girths, ease off their saddles and walk their ponies round to cool them off before they took them back to the box.

Simon and Zodiac were covered in mud when they rode through the finish, and had obviously had a fall.

"Are you all right?" demanded Mrs Blair.

"It was the drop out of the wood," Simon told them. "She took a huge leap and I came off over her head. But I'm fine. Honestly. Zodiac slipped but she didn't come right down. All I was thinking about was holding on to my reins so we could jump the rest of the course. I wasn't a bit scared. Just felt like I used to before Merlin and I crashed."

"Well done," said Mrs Blair.

"Brill," said Thalia.

Simon slid to the ground.

"She's going to be a real cross-country pony," he said, clapping Zodiac's neck. "Even better than Merlin. The best I've ever ridden." And he was grinning from ear to ear.

Verity finished at a trot.

"Four refusals, and I think we've exceeded the time limit."

She was right. When the results were posted she had been eliminated. Simon's collection of penalty points put him at the bottom and Thalia, to her loud disgust, had been eliminated for taking the wrong course at the water jump. She had forgotten about the flags and jumped with the red flag on her left. Two eliminations meant that the team was out of the event.

But Sally was clear – no penalty points, no time points. A boy from the Haxton team was in second place, close behind Sally. If he jumped clear in the showjumping and Sally had a jump down, he would be first.

Both Thalia and Verity were allowed to take part in the showjumping but not allowed to compete. Waiting for her turn Thalia schooled Tarquin. She was maddened and aching at being eliminated. Her fault, not Tarquin's.

She rode Tarquin into the ring at a steady trot and cleared all the jumps from a controlled canter.

And then it was Sally.

"This isn't me," she thought. "Not me having to jump for first place!" The Haxton boy had gone clear and if she was to be first Willow must go clear as well.

As Sally cantered Willow in a circle she heard the signal to start and she was filled with the same confidence she had felt all day. She wasn't perched uneasily on the saddle but was sitting close to her pony, able to think and plan as she rode the course.

Willow cleared the first three jumps up the side of the ring and turned to take the diagonal row of jumps – a double, a brush and a spread of poles. At the second part of the double Willow's timing was wrong and she had to stretch to clear it. Bending from her waist, her hands light on the reins, Sally went effortlessly with her pony.

They cleared the double and the brush, turned up the opposite side of the ring over two spreads and an upright and were galloping back across the ring at the last jump – a high brick wall. Willow's hind foot clipped one of the bricks. It trembled but stayed in place. They were round clear.

The team prizes were presented first. The cup went to the Haxton team. Then they called Sally's name as the individual winner.

"Well done, my dear," said the grey-haired man who was presenting the prizes. "Very well done indeed."

Sally took the cup and rosette, stuttering over her thanks.

"Not only has this young lady won a cup for herself, but her dog saved a little boy from drowning. I'm happy to tell you that he is now home in bed but I think Sally Lorimer deserves another round of applause."

Sally sat numbly, staring into space as the burst of clapping swirled about her.

Not me, this isn't me, Sally thought. But it was.

When at last the ponies were loaded, Sally managed to escape from the congratulations, the praise and the curious questions from Pony Club mothers who wanted to find out who she was, and climb up into the cabin of the horsebox with Thalia and Martine. She clutched her cup in both hands, still hardly able to believe her day.

They unloaded Buster and Zodiac at Ashdale and then drove on to Kestrels. The vet was standing in Kestrels' doorway.

"Oh, stop! Please stop!" cried Sally. "I must find out how Meg is."

Sally jumped down from the box, and to her utter delight, mattering far more than cups or rosettes, Meg came barking to meet her.

"She's all right," cried Sally, hugging Meg to her. "She's better? She's really better?"

"She's some dog," said the vet. "She's made it. Couldn't be better. I've seen them go on for years when these pills agree with them. She'll be on them for the rest of her days but I don't suppose anyone will be objecting to that."

"Can't thank you enough," said Mr Lorimer who had arrived home half an hour before Sally.

"Thank you," said Sally stroking Meg's head, feeling her alive and warm and well again. "Thank you very much indeed."

"I told your dad," the vet said to Sally. "I was speaking to the dog warden about your hound. I stitched her up when the two men had her. No question of her being aggressive. She's one of the nicest natured dogs I've known. Both men are off to work on the oil wells, so I expect they dumped her. Anyway she's your dog now."

Even when they had seen to their ponies and Willow had finished her feed and was pulling contentedly at her hay net, Sally could not bear to leave her. She wanted to stay with her; to relive in her mind the best day of her life.

"I'm starving," insisted Thalia. "Utterly empty. Do come on."

Sally took one long, last look at Willow, her pony, who had galloped and jumped so boldly and yet taken her sweetly through the dressage test. The best pony.

"You do realise," said Thalia as they walked towards Kestrels, "I am absolutely eaten up with jealousy. I'm concentrating on Tarquin's show-jumping. Martine said she was incredulous. And it does mean, now you're completely not nervous, we can jump at the big shows. Qualify for the Horse of the Year show! Anything, absolutely anything!"

Suddenly Sally thought about her crystal unicorn. All day it had lain safely in her pocket.

Fen was lying on the doorstep. When she saw them coming she uncoiled herself and – tail swinging, ears bright – came to meet them walking close to Sally's side.

Thalia pushed the kitchen door open, stood back, and Sally found herself in a room full of people – all her family, Narg, Mrs Blair and Verity, Simon and his father, Martine, Misty and Meg. The long kitchen table was loaded with food, with pies and cakes and trifles. Sally stared in blank amazement.

Her father held up his glass.

"To the winner," he said, smiling proudly at her.

"Not me," said Sally. "It was all Willow. She's the winner."